Ava and the Magic Tutu

By Sandi Bloomberg
Illustrated by Kevin Collier

Outskirts Press, Inc.
Denver, Colorado

Ava and the Magic Tutu
A dancer's tale

Outskirts Press, Inc.
http://www.outskirtspress.com

ISBN: 978-1-59800-248-5

Outskirts Press and the "OP" logo are trademarks belonging to Outskirts Press, Inc.

PRINTED IN THE UNITED STATES OF AMERICA

Dedication

This book is dedicated to my granddaughter Ava, who loves to dance.

This Book Belongs To:

_____

Acknowledgements

I want to thank my husband Jerry and my three sons Ronny, Lee, and Michael, for their continued support of all my creative endeavors. I also want to thank Kevin Collier for his colorful and whimsical illustrations.

Ava wanted to be a ballerina ever since she saw a production of "The Nutcracker" when she was five years old. When she was six, Ava's mother took her to Madame Grimble's School of Ballet. Madame Grimble gave Ava her first lesson. Ava was not very good.

"I can't do this. I can't do that. This is too hard!" grumbled Ava with each new position.

"Try it again dear," Madame Grimble said to Ava, but nothing worked. It seemed as though the little girl had two left feet.

"I don't like ballet," Ava said to her mother on their way out of the studio. "I don't want to go back."

"Will you try it one more time if I let you wear a special tutu?" asked her mother.

"What special tutu Mommy?" asked Ava.

"You'll see, dear, as soon as we get home," said her mother, as they got into the car.

When Ava and her mother walked into their house, Ava's mother ran down to the basement with her daughter following close behind.

There in a corner was a big old trunk with the key still in it. Ava's mother sat down in front of the trunk and began to open it.

"What's inside Mommy?" asked Ava.

"You'll see soon enough," said her mother. She lifted the heavy lid and Ava's eyes lit up.

The trunk was filled with beautiful costumes of lace, feathers and sequins in vibrant colors of red, gold and silver.

"These were your grandmother's costumes," said her mother. "She was a very famous dancer."

"Can I keep these costumes for dress-up Mommy?" Ava asked excitedly.

"Of course darling," said her mother, "But I want to find you something special at the bottom of the trunk."

They both took out costume after costume until they got to the very bottom, and there it was - The Magic Tutu!

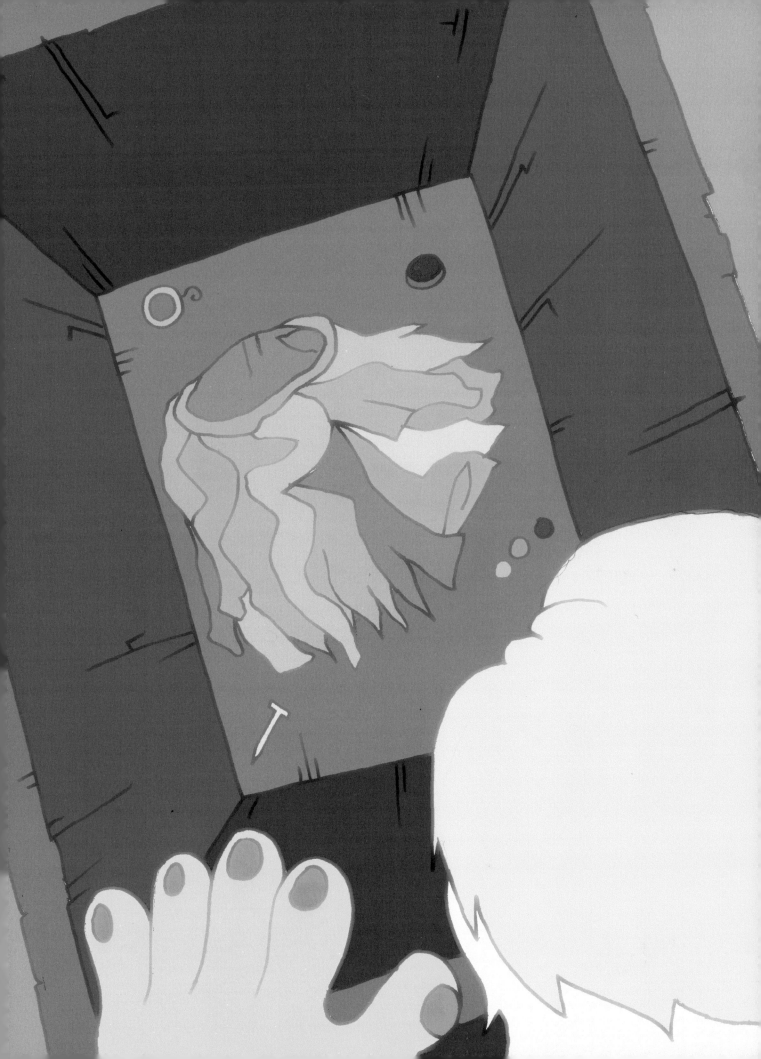

The small faded pink piece of chiffon was a little tattered in places, but fit Ava as if it were made to order.

"This was your grandma's tutu when she was your age and took her first ballet lesson," said Ava's mother.

Ava didn't even hear her words. As soon as she put on the tutu, she began to dance around the basement twirling and leaping as graceful as a gazelle.

"Oh, Mommy, I want to dance just like my grandma!"

"Will you let me take you back to Madame Grimble's class?" asked her mother.

"Oh yes, but only if I can wear my grandma's tutu" exclaimed Ava.

The next day when Ava entered the dance studio, the other little girls laughed at her wearing the faded, tattered tutu.

Their laughter soon turned to "oohs and aahs," as they watched Ava gracefully pirouette and leap across the floor.

Madame Grimble looked on in amazement. Wasn't this the little girl with two left feet she had seen yesterday?

"Ava," she said, "You were just fooling me. You have had many lessons before."

"No Madame Grimble, yesterday was my very first lesson, but today I have on my grandma's tutu. She was a very famous dancer, and I'm going to be just like her."

Madame Grimble asked Ava's mother who the famous grandmother was, and when Ava's mother told her, Madame Grimble almost fainted.

Ava's grandmother had been one of the most famous ballerinas in the world. Every dancer knew of her.

"Now I know why Ava can dance so beautifully," said the excited Madame Grimble. "She will most certainly follow in her grandmother's footsteps!"

Ava wore her Magic Tutu to every class, and soon had all the leading roles in Madame Grimble's ballets.

Ava's grandmother would have been very proud of her. In fact, she had planned it just this way.

What Ava didn't realize, was that she could dance even without the Magic Tutu.

Sometimes your self-confidence needs a little help, and when you believe in yourself, anything is possible!

CPSIA information can be obtained
at www.ICGtesting.com
Printed in the USA
LVIC080433271112

308939LV00004B

9 781598 002485